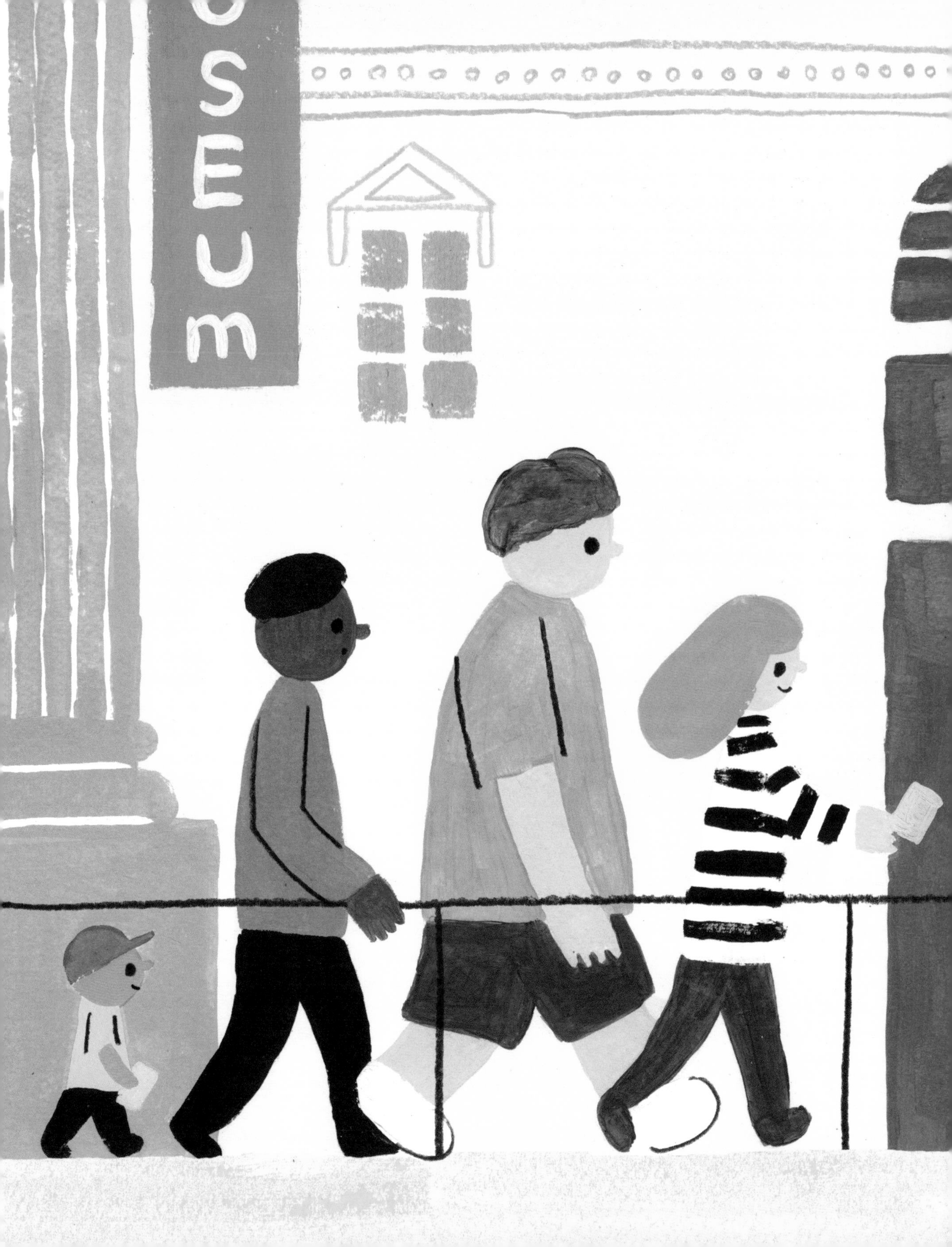
USEUM

© 2017, Prestel Verlag, Munich · London · New York
A member of Verlagsgruppe Random House GmbH
Neumarkter Strasse 28 · 81673 Munich

Prestel Publishing Ltd.
14 –17 Wells Street
London W1T 3PD

Prestel Publishing
900 Broadway, Suite 603
New York, NY 10003

Library of Congress Control Number: 2017938209
A CIP catalogue record for this book is available from the British Library.

Project management: Doris Kutschbach
Production management: Corinna Pickart
Separations: Reproline Mediateam, Munich
Printing und Binding: DZS Grafik, d.o.o., Ljubljana
Paper: Tauro

Verlagsgruppe Random House FSC® N001967

Printed in Slovenia

ISBN 978-3-7913-7319-5
www.prestel.com